Joyride

Lauren Myracle

D0067742

SCHOLASTIC INC.

New York   Toronto   London   Auckland   Sydney
Mexico City   New Delhi   Hong Kong   Buenos Aires

**Illustrations
Ben Shannon**

3 1969 02094 8609

Developed by ONO Books in cooperation with Scholastic Inc.

ISBN 0-439-57921-X

1 2 3 4 5 6 7 8 9 10   23   12 11 10 09 08 07 06 05 04 03

Contents

Welcome to This Book

Would you do anything to help a friend who was in danger? What if it meant facing danger yourself? Would you dare?

Nory's been friends with Thomas for as long as she can remember. Now Thomas may be in big trouble. Nory thinks he's been kidnapped and taken to another planet. Nory has to save Thomas, but how? To help him, she'll have to face her worst fears—and overcome them!

Will Nory be brave enough? Can she find her courage in time to save Thomas?

Target Words

These words will help you understand Nory's big adventure.

- **cautious:** careful

  Nory is a cautious person who doesn't take risks.

- **mocking:** in a way that makes fun of someone

  The bully's mocking laughter hurt Nory's feelings.

- **transformation:** a complete change

  Thomas's transformation turned him into someone very different.

Reader Tips

Here's how to get the most out of this book.

- **Subtitles** Subtitles, or teasers, give you a hint of what will happen in the chapter. Look at the beginning of Chapter 1–"The Dare" on page 6. What does the subtitle, "Will Nory take a space shuttle out for a spin?" tell you about what might happen in this chapter?

- **Problem/Solution** Nory faces many problems during the course of the story, but what is the main problem she has? While you read, try to follow the actions she takes to solve this problem. How is she able to find a solution by the end of the story?

1

The Dare

Will Nory take a space shuttle out for a spin?

"Chicken! Nory is a chicken!" Stockton and Bruce had cornered Nory the moment they spotted her. They were teasing her because she wouldn't take one of the space shuttles out for a ride.

"Listen," Nory said. She tried to act tougher than she felt. "I couldn't take a space shuttle out if I wanted to. The system is locked."

"Actually, Bruce **hacked** into the system," Stockton said.

"It was easy," Bruce said. "All the adults can think about is Carnival. I messed with the computer controls. No one even noticed."

"So there's nothing stopping you," Stockton said to Nory. "Unless you're afraid of the dark. Is that it?"

Stockton and Bruce cracked up. Nory dug her fingernails into her palm. Why couldn't they just leave her alone? Stockton and Bruce bullied her all the time. No grown-up ever stepped in. That was the way it worked on the space station. Once you turned fourteen, you had to solve your own problems. You didn't ask for help.

Nory heard footsteps on the deck. A familiar voice called out, "Nory? You up here?"

Nory breathed a sigh. It was Thomas. "By the shuttles," she answered.

Thomas came into view. He was wearing his red ball cap. Nory smiled, glad to see her friend.

Thomas grinned back at her. Then he looked at Stockton and Bruce. He stepped between them and Nory.

"Ho, Stockton," he said. "Ho, Bruce. What's so funny?"

"Your girlfriend is too chicken to take out one of the shuttles," Stockton said.

Nory blushed.

"She's not chicken," Thomas said. "She's just got better things to do. Like go to Carnival with me. Right?"

"It's just a bunch of freaks from other planets." Stockton said. "What's the big thrill?"

"You're the freak," said Thomas. Then he grabbed Nory's hand "Come on Nory. Let's go."

As they headed toward the Great Hall, Nory looked at Thomas's face. He was grinning in **anticipation.** Thomas loved excitement. He had always been that way. It was one of the things Nory really liked about him. And it never seemed to bother him that Nory would rather watch from the sidelines. Nory had asked him about it once. He had shrugged his shoulders and said, "Some people do great things. Others think up the great things to do."

Nory had laughed. He was right. She did think up most of the wild things Thomas did. She once told Thomas how a person could crawl straight from the boys' wing to the girls' wing through the

---

Heads Up!

Nory is thinking back to adventures that happened in the past. In a story, that's called a flashback.

Stockton and Bruce stop picking on Nory once Thomas shows up.

air **ducts.** And Thomas actually did it. Another time she told Thomas how to work the **air locks,** and he went for a space walk outside of the station. He had come back grinning from ear to ear.

Sometimes Nory wished that she could be more like Thomas. But mostly, she was just glad that he was her friend. Stockton and Bruce were right. She was chicken. But with Thomas around, she could ignore their **mocking** laughter.

Heads Up!

What kind of friend is Thomas? How would you describe his friendship with Nory?

Carnival

All the aliens are here.
And Dame Steel is the creepiest of them all.

Carnival was only held once every five years. Creatures from all the nearby planets were there. Everyone brought products to sell and trade.

Nory had been nine when the last Carnival was held. No one under thirteen was allowed inside. So, this was Nory's first time. She stood with Thomas and stared.

Buldwins from the icy planet of Arctacia sweated at their booth. Their thick fur was too warm for this climate. Plus, they had three heads apiece. That meant three times the complaining. And they were loud.

The long-necked Zaggats across the way looked like they were getting annoyed at the Buldwins. Nory hoped a fight wouldn't break out.

Suddenly, Thomas grabbed Nory's arm.

"Nory, look over there!" he said. "Is that who I think it is?"

Nory followed his gaze. At a booth all by herself stood a tall woman. Her skin was gray and her lips were blue. She wasn't smiling.

"Dame Steel," Nory said in a stunned voice. "It has to be."

Dame Steel lived on the planet Elektra. On Elektra, everything was made of metal. Even Dame Steel's heart was made of metal. People said it was an **experiment** that went wrong.

They said she did other experiments, too, and not only on herself. Many people were afraid of her. They tried to get Dame Steel banned from Carnival. She was dangerous, they claimed.

But the law said everyone of age was allowed to attend Carnival. And that included Dame Steel.

"Let's go check out her robots," Thomas said. "I've heard they're really lifelike."

"Thomas, no," Nory said. "You know what people say."

Thomas looked at her in a way that made her feel silly. "Grown-ups tell those stories to scare kids," he said. "But we're not kids anymore. Come on, Nory."

Nory didn't move.

Thomas sighed. "Well, let's meet for the feast at seven, then. Deal?"

Nory nodded as Thomas walked away. As she watched him, she felt tight inside. Suddenly, she made a decision. She was not going to be a watcher for the rest of her life. She stood up straight. She started for Dame Steel's booth.

Nory was amazed by the robots on display. She saw dancing dog robots. She saw singing bird robots. And there were many more. All were tiny. All of them clapped or sang or marched. To Nory, they didn't seem lifelike at all. They seemed terribly sad. They looked like all the life had been sucked out of them.

As she got closer, she saw something strange. She saw Dame Steel pick up a robot to show

—Heads Up!——

Do you think Nory has good reason to be afraid of Dame Steel? Why or why not?

Thomas. It was shaped exactly like a boy, only much smaller.

Thomas took the boy robot in his hands. On its chest was a switch. Thomas looked up at Dame Steel. Dame Steel nodded, and Thomas flipped the switch. There was a hissing sound. Sparks flashed in the air.

Thomas jerked back. "Ow!" he said.

Nory's heart leaped to her throat. "Thomas!" she cried. "Are you all right?"

Thomas and Nory look at one of Dame Steel's robots.

Dame Steel

What's come over Thomas?

"Whoa," Thomas said. "I must have gotten a shock. It hurt like crazy. But only for a second. I'm fine now."

"Are you sure?" Nory said. She reached to touch his arm.

Thomas pushed Nory's hand away. "I said I'm fine!"

Nory stepped back. She was startled by Thomas's tone. It sounded mean.

"Is this one of your friends, Thomas?" Dame Steel asked.

"Yeah, this is Nory," Thomas said. "She didn't want to come over. She was afraid you might use her in one of your experiments." He laughed in a way that was not very nice.

Nory was confused. Why was he acting this way?

"Some people do fear me," Dame Steel said. She narrowed her eyes at Nory.

"Not me," said Thomas.

"That's because you **appreciate** my creations," Dame Steel said. She put her hand on his shoulder. "They're quick. They're clever. They are not limited by feelings. And they would never be held back by something as foolish as fear."

Nory's face grew hot. She wanted to say something to prove Dame Steel wrong. She wanted to show she wasn't afraid.

Instead, she turned to Thomas. "Let's go," she said under her breath. "I'm getting really creeped out."

"Why am I not surprised?" Thomas said. "Quit being such a baby."

Nory felt as if she'd been slapped. She stared at Thomas. Then she turned and ran from the hall.

Heads Up!

Reread what Dame Steel says to Thomas about her creations. What does this tell you about her?

17

Ditched

Would Thomas really ditch Nory?
Or was something else going on?

Alone in her room, Nory fought back tears. Why was Thomas being so mean to her? He had always stood up for her. He'd protected her when others made fun of her. Now, he was the one making fun of her. But why? Had he finally gotten tired of her being such a wimp?

No, she told herself. They'd been through too much together for her to believe that.

It was true that sometimes he teased her for being so **cautious.** But his teasing had always been in fun. Surely that was true this time, too. Thomas was just showing off for Dame Steel. Nory wouldn't make a big deal out of it.

She got off her bunk bed. She dragged a brush through her hair. The opening feast was about to begin. Thomas would be looking for her. She would go and find him. At least she could ask him what was going on. Then he could explain.

Nory went back to the Carnival. But Thomas was nowhere to be seen. She went back to Dame Steel's booth. But it was all packed up. How strange. As Nory wondered what this could mean, someone shoved her from behind.

"Looking for Thomas?" Bruce said.

Nory turned to go. But Stockton was blocking her path.

"Sorry, Nory," he said. "But it looks like you've been ditched."

"What are you talking about?" Nory said.

"Thomas left. With Dame Steel."

"Thomas wouldn't do that," Nory said. But she wasn't so sure now. She felt her stomach dip.

"Whatever," Bruce said.

Stockton smirked, and Nory pushed past him.

Nory almost fled back to her room. After all, Thomas clearly didn't care about her. So why should she care about him?

But something didn't feel right.

Maybe Thomas had ditched her. Maybe this was his way of brushing her off. Or maybe something else was going on.

Maybe it was something worse.

Heads Up!

If you were Nory would you be worried about Thomas? Why or why not?

Three, Two, One—Blast Off!

Nory takes that ride after all.

"Thomas?" Nory called. "Thomas!" She stopped everyone she saw, every human and every other creature, too. "I'm looking for a boy my age," she told them. "He's wearing a red ball cap. Have you seen him?"

The answer was always no.

Nory scrambled up the ladder to Deck Two. That's where the shuttles were docked.

"Thomas?" Nory called. Her voice echoed in the empty hall. "Are you here?"

She scanned the shuttle dock. Something on the floor caught her eye. Something red. It was Thomas's hat. **Dread** washed over Nory. Thomas never went anywhere without his cap. Why was it lying on the floor? Had Thomas gotten on a shuttle with Dame Steel?

Nory wanted to run for help. But she knew there wasn't time. She'd have to deal with this herself. She had to go after Thomas.

She picked up Thomas's hat and jammed it on her head. Maybe it was stupid, but she wanted it with her. Then she went up to the computer controls. Her heart was pounding. Did Stockton and Bruce leave the system unlocked? She wiped her hands on her jeans and placed one palm on the screen.

"Shuttle requested," she managed to say. The computer buzzed. The door to Shuttle 5-A slid open. It was as easy as that.

Nory climbed aboard. The computer asked for her **destination.** Nory gulped. "Elektra," she said.

Nory strapped herself into her seat. The computer began the countdown. Then the shuttle took off into space.

At first, Nory felt dizzy. With zero gravity inside the craft, everything felt different. Things started floating around the shuttle. Up was no longer up. Down was no longer down. If she hadn't been strapped in, she would have been floating, too.

Thomas would love this, she knew. But Nory felt sick to her stomach. "I'm doing this for him," she reminded herself. "He better be worth it."

Hours later, the shuttle landed with a jolt. Nory undid her straps with trembling fingers. She started to open the door. Then she stopped. She'd never traveled to another planet before. She had no idea what to expect. She knew from her studies that Elektra was a Class One planet. She knew she'd be able to breathe the air. But that was about all she knew.

Would she be attacked the second she stepped outside? Or would she step onto a spooky and abandoned planet?

She was about to find out.

Heads Up!

What clue makes Nory think that Thomas has been taken on a shuttle to Elektra?

CHAPTER

Welcome to Elektra

It's not the kind of place you'd pick for a vacation. But Dame Steel calls it home.

The first thing Nory saw was the shine of metal. There were no trees, no plants, no flowers. Just chunks of metal. They stretched from the shuttle to the **horizon.** Then she heard something behind her. She whipped around.

"Ahhh!" she screamed.

It was an enormous bird with a broad body and a round head. His eyes were dark. His feathers were white. He was bigger than Nory herself.

The bird's eyes widened. He stumbled backward. "Oh, me. Oh, me!" he **twittered.** "Oh goodness me!"

Nory's heart raced. She started to duck back into the shuttle. Then she saw that the creature was waddling off. She could hear him hooting

24

under his breath. Suddenly, it was hard to be frightened of this overgrown owl.

"Wait!" Nory called. "I'm new here, and—" She realized she didn't know what to say. "I'm Nory. What's your name?"

The bird turned back. He looked at Nory. Nory tried to look relaxed. She wanted the owl to think that she traveled to strange planets all the time.

"Are you . . . a girl-child?" the bird asked.

For a second, Nory was **offended.** She wasn't a child. But to the bird, everyone probably looked small, like a child.

"I guess so, yeah," she said.

"And are you a friend of Dame Steel?" he demanded. "Are you, are you?"

"No!" Nory exclaimed. "Not even!"

The bird calmed down. He smoothed his wings. Nory saw that they were made of metal. Then he puffed out his chest. "Then welcome. I am Blaylock. I welcome you to Elektra."

"Er . . . thank you," Nory said. Then she told Blaylock about Thomas. She explained how he had met Dame Steel at Carnival. And then suddenly he was gone.

Nory tells Blaylock about Thomas and Dame Steel.

"I'm afraid something really bad has happened," she finished.

Blaylock nodded. "You're right to be afraid. Oh, yes. Very, very."

"What do you mean?" Nory asked.

"I used to be the finest Oolat in the land," he said. He flapped his wings. "But what use are metal wings? What use, what use?!"

"You mean you can't fly anymore?" Nory said. "You've tried? The wings don't work?"

Blaylock squawked and flapped his wings again. "I don't have to try! I know!"

Nory blinked. She hadn't meant to upset him.

"What she did to me, she'll do to your friend," Blaylock warned. "Oh yes, just wait. She'll turn his legs into iron. Or his heart to steel. And when the change is complete? Oh dear, oh dear. The Thomas you know will exist no more."

This was exactly what Nory had feared most.

Heads Up!

What does the planet Elektra look like? What kind of creatures do you think live there?

But hearing it said out loud made her mad. Dame Steel wasn't going to get away with it. Nory would make sure of that.

"Take me to Dame Steel's lab," she demanded.

Blaylock stepped backward. "No, no. Oh, absolutely no."

"Oh, yes," Nory said firmly. "And hurry, or we'll be too late."

―Heads Up!―――――――

How would you describe Blaylock? In what ways is he like Nory?

Attack of the Rovers

Will a giant cockroach keep Nory as a pet?

Nory walked quickly to keep up with Blaylock. He headed west and led them over a rocky hill. As they came down on the other side, Nory saw that there were trees on Elektra. They were twisted trees with metal branches. Where the metal met the bark, the bark was sliced and torn. Looking at them made Nory shiver.

Nory and Blaylock entered the gray forest. As they walked, Nory asked about Dame Steel. Blaylock told her all he could.

She wasn't always such a monster, he said. But long ago she'd fallen in love. Her love wasn't returned. So she began to experiment with metal. Metal has no feelings. She used it to harden her heart. She turned her heart to steel so that she'd never love again.

"Well, fine," Nory said. "If that's what she wanted to do. But why did she mess with you? And why Thomas?"

"Not just us," Blaylock said. "Every living creature she meets."

"Yeah, but why?"

"She says it's to make us better," Blaylock said. "But I know the truth. Since she can't feel love, she doesn't want anyone else to, either." He clucked and shook his head. "I'm lucky I escaped when I did. Oh yes, I am, I am. Only my wings are metal. Inside, my heart is still me."

They traveled deeper into the forest. Suddenly, Blaylock's body tensed.

"What's wrong?" Nory asked.

Blaylock turned his head from side to side. He flapped his metal wings and screeched. "Rovers! Oh, dear! Oh, dear! Run for your life!"

Heads Up!

What happened to change Dame Steel? Describe in your own words why Dame Steel turns creatures to metal.

Blaylock fled. He left Nory alone in the woods. She didn't have time to think before two arms wrapped themselves around her. Or was it four arms? Or six?

She twisted to see what held her. Then she wished she hadn't. It looked like a giant metal cockroach. Its legs were shiny and sharp. They were tipped with steel blades.

"Get off me!" she yelled. She struggled. The Rover tightened its grip.

"We'll feast tonight," it hissed. It raised a blade to Nory's throat.

"No, Da!" a smaller Rover said. "Me want!"

The big Rover laughed. Then it shoved Nory forward. "You want? You take. You no want it later. Then we feast!"

The smaller Rover moved forward. It pulled Nory close. It stroked her cheek. "Me Kank," it said. "Daughter of Tern. You who?"

"Let go of me, and maybe I'll tell you," Nory said. Kank's breath smelled awful, like rust and dead rodents.

Kank spotted Thomas's red ball cap. She reached for it with one of her six arms.

Kank keeps Nory for a pet.

Nory pulled away. "No!"

Kank giggled. But she didn't take the hat. "You mine now," she said. "My thingie. Come!"

Kank pushed Nory along a path through the woods. Soon they reached the Rover camp. It looked more like a garbage heap. Nory saw piles of scrap metal mixed with bones. She shuddered.

Kank showed her the tents where the Rovers lived. Behind the tents was a pen full of animals. The animals were short with wide backs. They had long hair that was tangled and dirty. They looked very ugly and very sad.

"Urgs," Kank said. She ducked under the fence. "Watch."

Kank raised a leg to one of the Urgs' throats. She ran her blade under the Urg's neck. "Tickle, tickle," she said. The Urg made a noise like a frightened horse. Kank laughed. "I scare. Ha!"

Nory bit her lip and turned away.

Kank ducked back under the fence. "Now sleep," she said. She led Nory to a dirty tent and shoved her inside.

She pushed Nory down. Then she lay next to her. She pressed up close.

Nory could hear Kank breathing. She could feel Kank's sharp blades through her T-shirt. She stared into the darkness for what seemed like hours. At last she fell into a troubled sleep.

Heads Up!

What details help create a frightening picture of the Rovers?

An Even Trade

Nory makes a deal with Kank.

Nory woke up stiff and aching. Kank was snoring next to her. One of her legs was thrown over Nory's shoulder.

Carefully, Nory eased out from under Kank's leg. She tiptoed toward the tent's flap. Then she heard a scraping sound as Kank moved to block her path.

"Oh no, my thingie," Kank said. "You stay with Kank forever!"

Nory blinked back tears of frustration.

Kank frowned. "Thingie unhappy?" she asked. "Why?"

"Because I've been captured by a giant cockroach!" Nory wanted to say. But she didn't. Instead, she tried to calm down. She placed her hand on Kank's cold steel body.

"I am your friend," she said.

"Yes! Thingie Kank's best friend!"

"But I have another friend, too," Nory said. "His name is Thomas. He's in danger."

Kank frowned. "Danger everywhere."

"Yeah, but Thomas needs my help," Nory said. She told Kank the full story. Kank listened closely. She hissed at the mention of Dame Steel.

"No more Thomas," Kank said. "Dame Steel took him? He gone, all right. Dame Steel did this to us." Kank lifted a metal leg to show Nory.

"But I can't just forget about him!" Nory said.

"Sure, you can," Kank said. She closed her eyes. Then she opened them. "See? Thomas all gone. Poof!"

Nory shook her head. "I have to go to Dame Steel's lab," she said.

Kank's face fell. "No, my thingie. Then I be unhappy. Nory no go."

Nory **hesitated.** Then she took off Thomas's red ball cap. "I'm going to leave, one way or another. If you help me, I'll give you this."

"For mine?" Kank said. "Forever?"

Nory nodded. Kank snatched the hat.

"Come," she said. "Before Da wakes up."

Kank led Nory to the pen behind the tents. She untied an Urg and told Nory to climb on. Then she gave Nory a chunk of meat. She gave her a skin bag filled with water as well.

"See river?" Kank said. She pointed through the trees. "Lab is on other side." She slapped the Urg's rear to get it moving. "Go."

Heads Up!

Nory says she's Kank's friend. Is she telling the truth or not? How does she get Kank to let her go?

The Lab

Finally, Nory makes it to Dame Steel's door.
Does she have the guts to go in?

The Urg moved quickly. Nory held tight to its rough **mane.** As she rode, she saw something in the woods. She wasn't sure what. But it seemed to be moving at the same speed as she was. Whatever it was, it kept to the shadows.

After several hours, the Urg reached the river. On the far side stood a huge steel building. It had no windows. Its smooth walls shone in the sun. It hurt Nory's eyes to look at.

"Is that it?" she asked. "Is that the lab?"

The Urg grunted. It dumped her off its back. Then it took off to the west and was gone.

"Great," Nory said. She stared at the river in front of her. It was deep and wide. "What am I supposed to do now?"

Just then something came out of the woods. It was big. It was white. And it had metal wings.

"Blaylock!" Nory exclaimed.

"I'm a terrible coward," Blaylock said in his fluttery voice. "I know, I know. But I can help you cross the river. Will you let me, girl-child?"

Nory ran to Blaylock and hugged him. "You are not a coward," she told him. "A coward wouldn't be here now."

Blaylock bent down, and Nory climbed on. He waded into the river. Nory clung to his feathers.

"We have to come up with a plan," Nory said. "If we stick together, we can do this. We can save Thomas from Dame Steel."

Blaylock stumbled. Cold water splashed onto Nory's leg.

"Blaylock?" Nory said. "Is something wrong?"

"Not a thing, not a thing," he said. But Nory heard the worry in his voice.

"Blaylock," Nory said again.

He shook his head. "I've been caught by Dame Steel once. I can't risk being caught again. I'm sorry, I'm sorry, But you'll have to face her alone!"

Nory felt her courage draining away.

They reached the other side of the river. Nory slid to the ground. The lab stretched high above her. The **jagged** metal on top tore into the sky.

"I can't," she whispered to herself.

"What's that?" Blaylock said. "Changed your mind? Yes, yes. I certainly understand." He looked at the lab and clucked. "We better get going then. Hurry, now. Back up you go."

Nory looked across the river at the woods. Its poor, twisted trees seemed to cry out to her. She looked in front of her at the lab. Somewhere inside was Thomas.

"Nory?" Blaylock said.

If she didn't save Thomas, no one would. She didn't say a word. She headed for the lab.

Heads Up!

Blaylock is afraid of Dame Steel. But do you think he's a coward? Why or why not?

Here, Kitty Kitty

Can Nory turn a couple of wild beasts into kittens?

Two guards stood outside the lab's entrance. They were metal tigers with silver stripes. Tiny cameras had been placed where their eyes once were. Nory heard a whirring sound as they looked over the area.

Nory didn't know what to do. She had to get past the guards to reach Thomas. But how?

She stepped into view. The guard beasts spotted her. One of them growled. Then it pounced. It knocked Nory down and put its paws on her shoulders.

"What is your business?" it snarled.

Nory thought fast. "I heard that Dame Steel created the most **marvelous** creatures in the universe. And looking at you, I believe it's true."

41

The beast took its paws off of Nory. She scrambled to her feet.

"You think we're marvelous?" the beast said.

"Oh, yes," Nory said. She remembered her dorm mother's cat, back on the space station. She remembered how **vain** it was. She remembered, too, how it liked to be petted.

"May I touch you?" she asked. "Oh, metal fur! And those stripes! Are they made of tin?"

The beast sniffed. "Aluminum," it said, as if that should have been obvious. But it let Nory place her hand on its back. Nory stroked the beast from head to tail. The beast **arched** its back. A rusty purr started up in its chest.

Then the other beast came forward. It nosed Nory's hand. Nory scratched the metal behind its ears and under its chin.

"And you're a beautiful beastie, too," said Nory. "Two such beautiful beasties." She paused for a moment, then said, "May I go in the lab? I know the other creatures won't be as marvelous as you. But just the same, I'd like to see them."

"Which of us is more marvelous?" asked the first beast.

"Yes. Which?" asked the second beast.

They were blocking the entrance.

Oh great, Nory thought. Now I'm never going to find Thomas.

"Um—I'll have to think about it. When I come out, I will tell you who is the most beautiful beast of all," she said.

To Nory's surprise, the beasts rubbed against her and purred. Then they moved back and let her walk towards the entrance. She swung open the heavy metal door.

As she stepped inside, she heard one of the beasts say, "I am more beautiful."

"No, I am," said the second beast.

Nory sighed. She would deal with them on the way out—if she made it out!

Heads Up!

Nory has had to talk her way out of two dangerous situations. How did she do it this time?

The Transformation

Nory finds Thomas. But is it too late?

Nory padded softly down the hall. Lights glared from the ceiling. The walls and floors gleamed as bright as mirrors.

Nory looked into rooms as she passed. In the first one she saw piles of robot parts. A half-built robot slumped against the wall. It had a head and a body, but no **limbs.** Wires stuck out like snakes from its open joints.

In the next room, Nory saw a family of giant snails. Their shells were clear. Nory saw gears underneath. They traveled across the floor on shiny wheels. Back and forth, back and forth. The smallest snail had one wheel missing. It humped along after the others, trailing behind.

Nory kept walking. At the end of the hall, she came to a door. "**Transformation** in Progress," warned a sign. "Do Not Enter." Nory tried the knob. It turned in her hand.

The room she entered was darker than the others. It took her eyes a moment to get used to it. Then she saw a hunched shape on the floor. She moved closer. A sick feeling flooded her body.

"Thomas?" she said.

He was curled on the floor. His arms were wrapped around his knees. His eyes were open. But he didn't seem to see. His skin was gray. His lips were blue.

"Thomas!" Nory cried. She knelt and shook his shoulders. "It's me. Nory! It's me!"

Thomas stared blankly ahead. He didn't respond, even with Nory right there beside him.

Tears welled in Nory's eyes. She couldn't believe she had come this far—and for what? She was too late. Thomas was no longer Thomas.

Heads Up!

The sign on the door says, "Transformation in Progress." What do you think could be happening to Thomas in there?

In the past, she'd fallen apart when things got tough. Fallen apart or ran away. But not this time. Now a flash of anger burned through her. She lifted her chin.

"Is this really the best you can do?" she yelled at Thomas. "You're just going to give up? I thought I was the coward. But it turns out it was you all along! I'm not the one who's afraid. You are! Or else you'd do something, instead of lying there like a big, stupid lump!"

She was crying now, despite her anger. Or maybe she was crying because of it. Her tears came hot and fast. There was nothing she could do about it. They spilled onto Thomas's face. They ran into his eyes.

And then she saw his eyebrows move, just the smallest amount. Or did she imagine it?

"Thomas?" Nory whispered.

"Huh?" he said in a grouchy voice. He pushed himself up. "Nory? Is that you? What's going on? Where am I?"

"Thomas, you're all right!" Nory exclaimed.

"That's what you think," Thomas said. "I feel like someone's yanked my insides out. And you sitting there sobbing isn't helping, either. It's just like you to cry at a time like this!"

She **gaped** at him. "I can't believe you!" she said. "You think I appeared here just like magic? You think I'm crying because I'm too scared to do anything else? You have no idea—" Nory was so angry that she couldn't even speak.

Thomas saw how upset Nory was. His face changed. He looked confused. "Wait," he said. "Nory, I didn't . . . I mean, I never meant—" Then Thomas got a strange look in his eye.

Nory held her breath.

"It's the strangest thing," Thomas said. He rubbed his eyes. His cheek was still wet from Nory's tears. "It's like there are sparks shooting inside me. It feels like I was filled with wires. Only now they're shorting out. I know that sounds crazy, right?"

Heads Up!

Nory's tears help turn Thomas back into himself. But how? What do you think was happening inside Thomas?

Nory half laughed and half sobbed. She threw her arms around him and said, "It is crazy. It's crazier than you'd ever believe. But you're you again, aren't you?"

"Well, sure. Who else would I be?" Thomas said. The color was returning to his skin. "But I have a feeling that we should get out of here."

"I couldn't agree more," Nory said. She pulled Thomas to his feet.

"Where do you think you're going?" said a voice. Dame Steel strode into the room. "The transformation is still in progress!"

Loyal to the End

Can two kids and an Oolat beat Dame Steel at her own game?

"Run!" Nory yelled. She and Thomas darted past Dame Steel and raced down the hall. But Dame Steel was part machine. She had speed and strength that was more than human. She was gaining on them with every second.

They burst out of the lab. For a moment, Thomas was blinded by the sun. He tripped. The guard beasts turned to pounce on him. But when they saw Nory, they lifted their heads and bared their teeth in what passed for smiles. Nory gulped and pulled Thomas up.

"Stop!" Dame Steel commanded. "I said stop, you idiot boy! Don't you realize what you're giving up? You could have been perfect. You could have been like me!"

Up ahead Nory saw Blaylock. He was fluttering and hopping at the edge of the river. "Oh, my! Oh, my!" he screeched. "She's coming, coming, coming!"

Terrified, he started to wade through the water on his own.

"Blaylock, come back!" Nory cried.

For an awful moment, Nory thought Blaylock was going to keep going. But he didn't. He turned around. His eyes met Nory's.

What he saw must have given him courage. He came back for Nory and Thomas. They jumped onto his back.

"But what are we going to do now?" Nory asked. "Even you can't outrun her!"

Blaylock spread his metal wings. He flapped hard and pushed off the ground. He soared into the air.

"You're flying!" Nory exclaimed.

"Yes!" Thomas cried. He pumped his fist in the air. "We're out of here!"

Nory looked over her shoulder at Dame Steel. Her face was full of **rage.** So, Nory thought, she couldn't get rid of all her feelings, not even close.

Blaylock soars into the air.

Behind Dame Steel was her lab. It looked cold and **forbidding.** But Dame Steel would return to it. She would live there with her inventions. They couldn't think or feel. They would stay there with her. But she would still be alone.

Nory clung to Blaylock. Thomas, behind her, held tight to her waist. She felt the warmth of his skin and was glad.

Blaylock flew swiftly through the sky. He landed at the shuttle Nory had flown in on. Nory and Thomas slid to the ground.

Nory buried her face in Blaylock's soft chest feathers. She stroked his metal wings. "Good-bye, Blaylock," she said. "I'll miss you."

"I'll miss you, too, girl-child," he said. He held her close. Then he let her go.

Nory climbed into the shuttle. She slid into the pilot's seat. Thomas followed behind her.

Heads Up!

Look up forbidding *in the glossary. Why do you think Dame Steel's lab looks that way? Do you think she is happy there?*

"Wait a minute," he said. He seemed nervous. He looked around the empty **cockpit.** "Who's going to fly this thing? Don't tell me you actually—"

"Sit back and relax," Nory told him. She strapped herself into the pilot's seat. "I'll take care of everything."

Four hours later, Nory and Thomas arrived at the space station. They docked at the port, and Nory raised the door. She climbed out first, then Thomas. They'd only gone a few feet when they spotted Stockton and Bruce. Bruce's face was red and he looked upset.

"Stop calling me a wuss!" he was saying. "You take it for a spin if you're so brave!"

"I happen to have a sore arm, remember?" Stockton said. "No one can fly a shuttle with a sore arm!"

"Ho, guys," Thomas said.

Stockton and Bruce whipped around. They saw Shuttle 5-A at the port. Its engine made popping sounds as it cooled down.

"Hey, where did you guys come from?" Stockton asked. "Where have you been?"

Thomas grinned at Nory. Nory grinned back.

"Oh, nowhere," Nory said. "We've just been out for a joyride."

Heads Up!

How have the characters changed from the beginning to the end of the story? How has your opinion of them changed?

Glossary

air lock *(noun)* a small room or passageway with two airtight doors (p. 10)

anticipation *(noun)* the state of expecting something to happen (p. 8)

appreciate *(verb)* to like or value someone or something (p. 17)

arch *(verb)* to make a curved shape (p. 42)

cautious *(adjective)* careful (p. 18)

cockpit *(noun)* the room in which a plane, boat, or spaceship is steered (p. 53)

destination *(noun)* the place a person is traveling to (p. 22)

dread *(noun)* state of fearing something will happen (p. 21)

duct *(noun)* a pipe or tube that carries air or an electric power line (p. 10)

experiment *(noun)* a test to try out something new (p. 12)

forbidding *(adjective)* unfriendly (p. 52)

gape *(verb)* to stare with an open mouth (p. 47)

hack *(verb)* to enter a computer system or program without permission (p. 6)

hesitate *(verb)* to stop or pause before doing something (p. 36)

horizon *(noun)* where the surface of a planet and sky meet (p. 24)

jagged *(adjective)* uneven and sharp (p. 40)

limb *(noun)* an arm or a leg (p. 44)

mane *(noun)* the long thick hair on the head and neck of an animal such as a horse or lion (p. 38)

marvelous *(adjective)* causing surprise, wonder, or amazement (p. 41)

mocking *(adjective)* in a way that makes fun of someone (p. 10)

offend *(verb)* to make someone feel hurt (p. 25)

rage *(noun)* great anger (p. 50)

transformation *(noun)* a complete change (p. 44)

twitter *(verb)* to talk very quickly (p. 24)

vain *(adjective)* stuck up, conceited (p. 42)